AESOP'S FABLES BOOK CASSETTES

THE BOY WHO CRIED WOLF

You can read this book as you listen to the cassette tape which accompanies it.
Turn the pages when you hear the tone signals.

Story adapter: Denise Guynn   Illustrations: Vernon McKissack

SVE
SOCIETY FOR VISUAL EDUCATION, INC.

1345 Diversey Parkway, Chicago, Illinois 60614
A BUSINESS CORPORATION

Copyright © 1980 Society For Visual Education, Inc.   All Rights Reserved Throughout the World.

ISBN 0-89290-076-8   Dewey Decimal Number: 398.2

Printed in United States of America

In a small, friendly town lived a little boy. Each summer, the boy had a job to do. He would care for his father's sheep. He would take the sheep up into the mountains.

All summer long, the sheep would stay there. They would nibble the green grass. But there was one thing wrong. The boy had to watch the sheep all alone.

He stayed in a cozy cabin. He had a lot of food to eat. But the sheep were no fun to talk to. "This is such a bore," the boy sighed.

One day, the boy woke up very early. He looked down at the town below. "Gee, all those people are down there," he said. "Why should I be all alone up here?"

Then he started to yell. "Wolf! Help! Wolf!" he cried.
Far below, the people heard his cry. The boy's father
leaped out of bed. "My sheep are in trouble," he said.

The father jumped into his clothes. He ran up the path
to help his son. Men from the town came along, too. At
last they reached the top. The men saw the boy and the
sheep. But there wasn't a wolf in sight.

"You ran fast," the boy chuckled. "You look so tired."

"Where's the wolf?" his father asked.

"Wolf?" the boy said. "There is no wolf. I did that so I could talk to someone."

The father's face turned red. "But you told a lie," he said. "And you made us run all the way up here. Don't ever do that again." Then the father left with the other men.

"Well, that was fun," the boy said. "But now I'm all alone again." He went back to his sheep.

A few weeks later, the boy tried it again. "Wolf! Help! Wolf!" he cried.

The people thought a wolf was eating the sheep. Up the path they ran. When they got there, the boy was laughing. He had told a lie again.

"Ha, ha, ha," the boy giggled. "I fooled you."
His father was very angry. "Be careful, son," he said.
"Your lies might get you into trouble."

A few days later a real wolf came. The wolf jumped on a sheep. "Wolf! Help! Wolf!" the boy yelled. "Wolf! I'm telling the truth!"

The boy's father heard him. He thought the boy was playing again.

The boy waited and waited for help. But no one came.
By now, all the other sheep had run away. The boy was all
alone. He had to watch the wolf eat the sheep for dinner.
Then the wolf walked away.

"Oh, I wish I hadn't lied before," the boy said. He started to cry. He had learned his lesson. "Don't ever tell too many lies," he said. "No one will believe you, even when you are telling the truth."